NEW AS A WAVE
A RETROSPECTIVE 1937–1983

BOOKS BY EVE TRIEM

Parade of Doves (E. P. Dutton, 1946)

Poems (Alan Swallow, 1965)

Heliodora (The Olivant Press, 1967)

e. e. cummings (University of Minnesota American Writers Series, 1969)

The Process (Querencia Books, 1976)

Dark to Glow (Querencia Books, 1979)

Midsummer Rites (The Seal Press, 1982; in print)

Eve Triem

NEW AS A WAVE

A RETROSPECTIVE 1937–1983

edited by
ETHEL FORTNER

DRAGON GATE, INC.

ISBN 0-937872-24-5
ISBN 0-937872-25-3 (paperback)
Library of Congress Card Number 84-4171

2   4   6   8   9   7   5   3
FIRST PRINTING, 1984

Published by Dragon Gate, Inc.
914 East Miller Street
Seattle, Washington 98102

ACKNOWLEDGMENTS

Poems in Section II were first published in *The American Scholar, Beloit Poetry Journal, Blue Unicorn, Botteghe Oscure, Cathedral Voices, Chicago Tribune Sunday Magazine, Compass, Elizabeth, Emily Dickinson: Letters to the World, Epoch, Epos, Galley Sail Review, The Human Voice, Kavita, King County Arts, the laurel review, Light, Plucked Chicken, Poetry Northwest, Poetry NOW, Prairie Schooner, Puget Soundings, Quarterly Review of Literature, Seattle Magazine, Spectrum, The Spokesman, St. Andrews Review, Tiger's Eye, Voices, Wind,* and *Yankee.*

"It Was before the Dawn," "Concert, in Wartime," "The Witness," "The Exile Tells His Friends," "Dubuque (I)," "Tell fables, Lamp, O honey" (entitled "The Lamp, and Heliodora"), "The Hostage," "Trees, Near and Far," and "New as a Wave" (entitled "The New Man") appeared originally in *Poetry.*

"The Losing" (entitled "Bitter It Was to Me") appeared originally in *The New York Times.*

Additional poems originally appearing under different titles are as follows: "Kings for Love" ("The Voyages of Dreaming"), *Quarterly Review of Literature;* "Am I Afraid?" ("Miracle Came to Me over Water"), *Botteghe Oscure;* "Love Is a Trinity" ("Nine Candles New Year's Eve"), *Yankee;* "Wake the Flute" ("Green Booth or Golden"), *Beloit Poetry Journal.*

Special thanks to Barbara Wilson, Rachel DaSilva and Seal Press for permission to reprint poems from *Midsummer Rites.*

Dragon Gate, Inc. joins the author in thanking the Western States Arts Foundation for both their publication award and their very kind and generous assistance.

CONTENTS

INTRODUCTION

So many poets, editors and friends have contributed to the publication of this book! My mother used to complain, "You have a thousand mothers!" My husband Paul said it better — "Little friend of all the world." Friendship is my life-style, whether it is a high school companion or beloved e. e. cummings. The Law of Admiration influenced my writing; sitting alone on the banks of the northern Mississippi River, twenty years in Dubuque, Iowa, I counted my idols: Shakespeare, Baudelaire, Federico García Lorca, Wallace Stevens, W. C. Williams, and Meleager.

What about the editors who befriended my poems? The late Harold Vinal, publisher of *Voices,* took some of my best lyrics, as did George Dillon of *Poetry* with whom I placed some of my best poems. The late Princess Marguerite Caetani, who edited *Botteghe Oscure* in Rome, wrote "Eve, the older you are, the more daring you get"; and Jean Burden, editor of *Yankee* Poetry page, was generous with praise. Carolyn Kizer, first editor of *Poetry Northwest,* has been a loving guide through the last twenty years. Have I forgotten the late Henry Rago, also editor of *Poetry?* Never! He was appreciative of my experiments and nested me in his heart. When I think of Theodore Weiss, publisher of *The Quarterly Review of Literature,* my joy mounts — he helped my poems to jump higher.

Speaking of books: the late Alan Swallow and the late D. V. Smith of Olivant Press both invited my manuscripts, with delightful results to my career. Then in 1976, to divert my attention from Paul's death, J. K. Osborne at Querencia Press created *The Process,* which contains many of my worthwhile poems. John Levy, his assistant editor, suggested, "So many people loved Paul, a chapbook of the published poems on his death would please them." Hence, *Dark to Glow.* Later, Seal Press offered to make a chapbook, so I sent them certain poems for which I had a sneaky fondness, but which I hadn't, for lack of space, included in other books. *Midsummer Rites* was the result. Thank you, Barbara Wilson.

So we come to the present moment, *New as a Wave*. Ethel Fortner, book editor at Olivant Press and a poet herself, labored long hours for this book. To the late Mimi Stewart McArdle, administrator of the Louisa Kern Fund, whose kindness provided a grant for typing, mailing, etc., the multiple versions of the manuscript, my gratitude. And to Kathryn E. Kaye, my wonder at her devotion and success in finding not only a publisher for the book but a prize!

Last, a credit to Joan Swift, book editor at Dragon Gate, Inc., my birthday twin. Our minds flow together. She restrained my gypsy impulses. Keats said, "Friendship is the holy emotion." Therefore, my love for Denise Levertov and Mary Randlett.

But I have mentioned my husband Paul Ellsworth Triem only in passing! I should give him credit for typing the envelopes when I said, "Let them publish me when I'm dead!" "Be a professional," said he. That internationally known writer, twenty years older than I, was a joy plus a bewilderment. Yet, without loving him I could not clash one verse against another. He said, "You party girl!" Yet he wooed me as I was. Bless him.

Eve Triem

Denise Levertov   Mary Randlett

O Athens, city of light, violet-crowned!
                                        (from Pindar)

PART I

from PARADE OF DOVES

PARADE OF DOVES

Your love is a parade of doves
tamed to courtyard corn
and marble bowls of water;
and they tread softly their own shadows.

How did I entice you
from your pine trees to my breast?
From what purer thirst
do you stoop to kiss my mouth?

If you left me now,
startled by the noise of my heart –
as if noon were invaded
by the dark hunger of owls,
and the songbirds were screaming –

I would crush all summer
like bergamot in my hands,
and go through the wrecked fields
crying:
"Have you seen a parade of doves
brighter than scattered corn,
and shining like water, when they fly?"

I THINK OF WAKEFULNESS

I think of wakefulness: if I were really awake –
not in the fringe of dreams, the human drowse,
the senses never quite waking –
what would I see when I looked at you:

A lake known only by night,
and now wide to the white flame of dawn, the dawn-wind
in the water-willows, the red-winged blackbird
triumphant as the dawn's voice,

or would you be the life of tansy and anise,
their serene flowering, their lemon and pungence
generous to any touch?

In a life never wholly awake, wholly alive,
what do we love?

I pray for wakefulness – with terror lest I wake –
and yet with joy.... Darling, I shall see at last
what sleepily I touched and blindly held!

4

LA NUIT IVRE

So this is the night the reveler sees,
Drunk and laughing under the trees,
Laughing and falling on the road
To home, in velvet to his knees.

A long, long way from gate and bed,
And falsely guided by overhead
Flaming of rose, green and amber
That will be burning when he is dead.

Oh lucky one, the way home lost,
Stumbling beneath the fragrance, tossed
Slowly from a tree half-waking
From the long nightmare of frost,

Laugh at the giant of your fright –
A shadow in a twist of light –
And sing – your throat against the moon –
How you discovered the true night.

LET COME THE GIVER

Tumult of space,
               break to nothing the heartless
In our wish: dark-amorous joy.
Dissolve us, acid moon, from our so
Self-centered selves; let come the giver,
In a quiet, after tumult, the generous
Outpouring like a pre-spring rain
To change the plunderer (who takes for all
Love as the perfume of white arms)
Into the giver, self-renounced,
Bewitching by this the acid moon
Into a given cup of milk.
(Sparkles of laughter in children's tears!)

Oh but the giver is shaken: love,
The perfume of white arms, bewitching...
Bewitching...

HIS OWN SONG

Jays in spring:
That robber-screech,
That din and clamor.
But jays can sing.

A jay,
Thinking he is alone,
Sings like a choir
Of all birds at dawn:
Robin and redbird,
Thrush-note, finch-note,
Each sound a savored word;
Then lets them float
Like water lilies on a wide lake
Into the bold light
Of his own song –
Marvel reserved for solitude:
Shine of the deep dream
About to wake
In the dreamed wood.

LET HIM PRAISE DEATH

Let him praise Death who meets
Her black brilliance for himself,
For whom she is hunger and fruit –
Venom his dream has sweetened.

But when she comes to steal,
Not him, but his darling,
Will he praise her, and seize
Her hair to bruise his mouth?

She will not leave him whole,
Nor wholly take him.
She will trample his herbs
And spill his blood's perfume,
And slash his dove's throat.
She will burn his earth's vineyard,
She will quench his earth's sun.

Now let him praise her –
From the night of scorched stone.
Naked to sleet and gale,
With tolling words,
With cries of lament
Let him praise Death
For her brilliant arms
And her breast obsidian.

A TAOIST PRINT

I feel the filament of life
tremble in my hands, and break.

The life in this print goes on forever.
Not mandarins or birds or princesses,
but, serenely, a wave, a moon, a cloud –
emblems
of immensities over man.
Immensities, loosening, re-tying
his bundles of small sticks....
Bewitched by emblems
he throws the sticks away.

And what remains?
"Creation without possession."
(O Lao-tse my brother!)
The comradeship of undemanding things,
Moon-rim, a falling wave, a lifted cloud.

moon-rim, a falling wave, a lifted cloud.

TO SING AGAIN THE VERSES OF HESIOD

Mist is the music enchanting these bricks
To move like awakened lions in their walls,
Like the bronzes and gold on the Shield of Herakles –

No longer a town blighting roses at noon; denying
To trees their dryads, to Apollo his tripods;
Nor a dusky town that shrines God, crucified.

Though we think bricks, and sheets on a line,
And mill-chimneys, are fixed forever to form,
The shape of things changes: there was the meadow-flax,

Going in fable from thread to cloth to paper, furious
For life each time; and every change was death –
But Death is a gate, and nothing is lost.

O rose-wreathed town, turning in a mist of roses
Sweet as a sunned cloth – though all the gods are dead,
Do you hear on your steep stairs the sandaled feet of Demeter?

THE MISSISSIPPI

Where is yesterday's river,
the virgin dancer in jewel-flame flood
and burning of turquoise at the bridge?

And there were swallows
cutting the glow
to make the sign for evening.

Corn-woman stream,
at once yellow ardor of harvest
and a meadow in spring.

Indian-woman water,
her rain-making rattles laid by,
so amorous-amber-still she lies
in the tawny lap of hills.
The weaned colt comes fearlessly,
the new lambs are fearless.

In the heat-glare of the red town,
water so indolent
that vigilant men forget
her Thunder-bird soul, flesh-sacrifice need,
and dazed by the fragrance of grain,
walk, reckless, her copper-coin waves.

CONCERT, IN WARTIME

The pianist thought he was driving a cart to market
the wheels careful
under the brilliant fruit and the wine jars.
Then the pianist thought he was running
with a waterfall in his arms,
stopping in this room
to lift from the chorded white of waters
the girl without a heart.

But these he imagined...
he was offering, really, a boy's head
on an airplane propeller:
he was shouting to the rustled programs
that these stained curls were beyond their kisses.
And he marched through the keys,
drumming that all fortresses were taken –
and no applause please.

THE WITNESS

Through a black and gold day, while the bright elm leaves
Fluttered by my window, larger than yellow butterflies,
And the gilded grasshoppers rose from brilliant grass,

Shapes fluttered by, shapes beckoned me through spaces between
Black stems of elms; their greaves, their shields were gleaming;
Their anklets clinked of gold, their crowns were tiered and shone.

Gods, and godlike men, they rose from the page,
The Greek lettering drifting round their feet — leaves of elm
In autumn. And I was their stunned and crying witness.

Through the black and gold fire of October
Flanked by flames in the mind — for the first bombs were fallen
        on Hellas —
I saw them, the golden of Homer, the bronze heroes of Aeschylus.

With voices of trumpets they told of survival,
How the smoke of book-burnings had left no reek in their hair,
Or stain on the gold, or dark in the heart.

Like the gentle telling of bells over water,
They pitied the races laboring with such fervor toward doom;
And they touched my mouth. And I was their stunned and
        crying witness.

IT WAS BEFORE THE DAWN

It was before the dawn.
                    The air between branches
was a river under evening:
aquamarine. Flax-flowers are like that,
and every dew-mirrored, wandering blue.
I was counting the sea-drowned boys, the fallen heaped in hollows;
the birds were beginning,
                    as if terror and sleep are twinned,
and they were waking.
They called from cliff to cliff
                    their unmelodic cries,
                    their ringing, clanged amazement.
To be alive, that was the wonder;
the sun, that was the reason.
They felt his heat
            as brooding feathers;
they heard the march through continental arches, the climb over
        the middle mountain.
And they cried in the vines,
and the air grew paler.
                    I held their voluble joy in my hand,
turned it like a coin, the inscription not to be read by me,
but the raised letters were real,
the curious figures, the interwoven crowns.
I turned to ask of the dead, if they knew:
They had gone, softer than perfume from old, shaken silk.
The day was in the room,
the hollyhocks were red,
and there were no more tears.

from POEMS

BETWEEN EARTH & HEAVEN

I

A yellowbrick school   below the city columns
      far below street level
and meshed with steel wire
where the railings used to be.

Almost noon
and white sunlight thickens
a paved yard.
The birdchattering women
                tilted on shiny heels
lean forward   they slant slim as incense sticks.
They seem to break
           inside their American clothes.

II

Between Earth & Heaven
the only sound alive
is a bell; many bells.
Bells simmer.
Then the slamming feet.

Skirts, and boys' red jackets –
the yard bursts into peony bloom.
The waiting women
revive
in that sugared fragrance.

III

No one is ashamed   of so much love
neither the grandmother – Cantonese –
who came too early,

> nor the black-eyed twins
> clinging
> to her damask sleeve.

THE EXILE TELLS HIS FRIENDS

As if he talked from a dream he is telling
of a square where the elms are topped with copper
red as the hair of sea-kings.   The mills.
Puffed from a millstack the slow dancers
bending black arms out of a sooty veil.

The telling becomes a singing: *A crag*
the waterworn feathers of that wing of stone.
Forgetting that once the town was his name for sorrow,
the roofs his blackened bones, the real bird dead.

                    Over that crag
a net of leaf-littered roads, a smell of leaves
like resins burned on a table of brass.

Tears on an old man's cheek. Lament in a dream.
Blue is a word cut in the stone of pain,
he does not remember why – telling and
telling of Indian weather ringing blue
a hundred bells. And the ringing stops.
And begins again in his wondering voice.

DUBUQUE (I)

Travelers notice this town for its bricks,
(warehouse and mill) sun-and-snow weathered
to apricot and dahlia.

And then that it is a port,
the streets in waves winding from a river
and flying the side of a hill, like gulls.

They will climb the star-sprayed hill –
the hill, a ballplayer's arm swung up for a catch
                          lost in the sun.
The townsmen below are as small as bees,
and as bright as bees
                          in their summer clothes.

Travelers notice,
steering their cars by elm-showered stoplights,
adding more boats, this might be Providence or Bangor:
cupolas, lookouts, widow-walks,
but for the glowing brick, the balconies,
the French-Provincial shape to the meanest houses.

It is New Orleans,
swept up from the Delta before the railroad time:
the black faces, the Creole place-names.

New Orleans, in the ironwork fencing the balconies,
a foliage of iron over the double glass doors,
wintry twigs of iron rimming the cornices.

For travelers
(missing the fighting cocks, the steeple pigeons)
the mills' steam whistles will startle
numerous jays into cornet calls;
will send them like a trellis of morning glories
into the thick of a pin-oak,
to drop for the reassurance of travelers
three clear notes
        like river-clam pearls.

LIKE THE BRAZEN GATES OF HOMER

Through a street of maples
you go
      glowing like the brazen gates
            of Homer.

From the green of a lopped pine
grackles grate their eerie farewells;
they float downriver
            in a plume of smoke.

You go through the streets like a cymbal choir,
and strangers untangle their hopeless thoughts to stop,
and then go slowly
            to that jubilant clang.

And you arrive at me....
The touch of porcelains, slowly, serenely watching
through a dust of crumbled time,
the warmth within the cling of virgin wool,
are in your look.

The day aflame with poignant marriages
of butterflies...the sulphur of their
            undefended wings...
the coming frost...are in your look of love.

NO ONE SHALL SLEEP

The young moon, like a luminous finger,
Points at sleep with its buried surprises;
The white and shockingly sweet nicotianas
Open their stars among the fireflies.

Surely we may sleep?
                    The night is tongued
With the yelp of dogs at every doorway;
Night is a river of laughing, brawling language.
And drunken laborers and love-drunk children
Wade. A cataract of cars
Falls all night, all through the lamp-pierced bell-plunged night;
All through the cloud-high clocks numbering the night.

They do not sleep....
                    Join the parade of phantoms,
The dead summers in their dead-gold garments,
The dead boys murdered by their dreams, the girls
Drowned in the loose hair of their useless longing.

Dance to the ghostly flute,
                    and in the choir
Of earth's ten thousand years of breeding ghosts,
Sing of Aidoneus, Death's kingdom's king,
Till the sun's paw
                    knocks the first star from the sky ...
And the radios begin.

LAND'S END

It is water
we came to hear
– gray,
        a radiance
underneath.

From an edge of the city –
        (hillside completely crusted
                with houses)
unravel the cypress trails
        patrolled by solitaries
        slender in jackets
        scattered like statuary.

And the shined waves
                stride high
        gray catching white.
        They trample at the rocks.

What we came for:
                an enlarging sound
                of our life
                        while we are alive.

AN EDGE, A SOLITUDE

There is an empire bearing my name
and thronged with doing for bitter and good.
What is least there a citizen
escapes to an edge, a solitude;
for emptiness of fist and heart
and a calm lawn of hopelessness
leaves the gold statues and brocades.
Finds a wide water. A simple voice.

A king selfbeggared is not bleak.
A lake for cup, a sky for wine.
White mountains clouded by whiter light
will shape a lamp, a crystal stain –
wasted in a birdquenching dusk,
a dusk I walk in streaming from me.
And from the world the great stars fade.
Then a bird over water shapes a star
and on that light I lay my head.

THE APPLES OF SILENCE

*There was a flower floated for a day
On a cactus-pool of green and spines;
And white and perfumed like the flesh of love.*

*And then a river – a Chinese vase
In tints of evening; the buff and henna hills
Arranged as phoenix-wing and magic vine.*

These moments are the ways, clear as a stone
When you turn it in the sun for veins of amber;
They are the roads to turn the mind toward silence.

But there are roads thicketed with loss,
Ways of craggy rock and anguished stumbles,
And weeping is the music in that mountain.

With *Silence* waiting like a crossways shrine
That every road approaches – the brilliant *Silence*
Melting the wry and wrong into its metal,

Within that inner *Silence* you are shining.

What does it mean? (As crumpled herbs have meaning?
As poppy seeds have a taste of sweet and strange?
As the cut wood has sides of smooth and shaggy?)

Like these, and more. It was the fruit of good –
The apples of God – that you ate in the dark.
The road back glows like ripe wheat with His love.

LEFTOVER ANGEL

Looked at, looked away from . . .
the bookcase has become invisible –
the top losing shape
in a keepsake clutter. Camel-bell and bullock-bell.
                    Dust on all, like a drowning.

Fogged sun, a dumb nonchalance.
The sun drops through a cloud.
            So high a room
            trembles in a traffic of winds,
            and rain hits the glass
            as a script of grace notes.

At the glow of a gull's shadow
the books came back,
and a wingless angel!
                    over the books –
            the doll-robe, green, medieval, the
                    walnut-shell lute;
            the features (in wax) of an aging peasant.

And this is an equivalent
of what happened on the road to Damascus:
            To look-and-to-see
            till the dust is wiped away.
            TO PAY ATTENTION. To care.
'Love is an energy, etc. . . .
is its own value . . .'

Bullock-bell and camel-bell
lengthening their tones
– (to be, know, and act,
infolded as one sound) –
into wings for the Angel.

from HELIODORA

from MELEAGER

My flowerful Heliodora, wear
the gay garland love has woven
for your curled and budded hair:

white violets, less white than you,
and lilies laughing like a summer
glistened with a daybreak dew.

Thinking of your kiss I chose
crocus and wine-dark hyacinth,
the silk narcissus, then the rose.

My sungift girl – Apollo's lyre
is less dear than your whisperings;
wear roses O my rose of fire.

And let the Graces have their fame.
By these petals I foretell
the lasting garland of your name.

from MELEAGER

Tell fables, Lamp, O honey
around Heliodora, lion
asleep on a mountain of bees,

girl I've sung of, sung
to; her sweets of speech a garland
Aphrodite wears in bed.

Her flowerful body (lute's garden),
Primavera's rosiest tunes
run there rivulets of wine.

No one but Meleager
shall *swan* it cozy under her
cloak; a sated god O withered

happy my night's roses scorching
in girl-lightning. For another,
drown your suns O Lamp; poppy

him sleepy helpless En-
dymion.... Does my lion
pounce from her honey-mountain,

mother of the Lamp, friendly night,
trap her glance. Does my lion claw
me to tears, keep them secret.

from AGATHIAS SCHOLASTICUS

My Heart, I am not fond of wine;
would you have me drunken, touch
lip to cup, and lift the cup to mine.

My better fortune, had I fled
the sweet cupbearer; if my wish
were a salty wit in sober head.

From the cup I take your kiss
and taste and cry unsoberly
that no wine held such loveliness.

from AGATHIAS SCHOLASTICUS

I

(O city, where are thy temples packed
with jewels that the fire had licked?)

Safer than weapons or walls could keep
did the watchman never sleep;

for the seawhite towers of home
rise in a lustered epigram.

Song sows the emptied field, recovers
the sober trees of gods and lovers.

Even her rosebud box the mighty
line returns to Aphrodite,

and offers Athene a bitter joy
in the undying name of Troy.

II

Accept my alms, O Heavenly Shield
of the city, let not your mind be numb
to the clang-cries of Ilium
dying into a blackened field.

Useless to your temple (O roof
as a sun in July) to bring my love.
The apple you are thinking of
puckers your heart, and you glide aloof.

Troy is no wolfish school for crime!
Better to let the cowherd Paris
be snatched to pieces by the Furies –
but God has fathered this flaming time.

from SAPPHO

Show me in a dream, Queen Hera,
your charming form that appeared once
at the prayer of the Atrêidai,
those godlike kings.

They completed the fiery doom of Troy
and left the Scamander. Homeward
they sailed but they could not
reach home

till they prayed to you, and potent Zeus,
and Thyone's winsome child. So again,
let me bring beauty to the maids
of Mytilene,

teaching them your songs and dances.
It was by your grace the renowned kings
left Ilium! Kind Hera, I beg you,
help my voyage.

from LEONIDAS OR MELEAGER

Death's freshest loot
's a honey-bee –
poets sing of me
      and Fate.

I sang, too,
collecting honey
though my sunny
      days were few.

Hell's greedy prince
likes sweet things most –
my wingless ghost
        laments.

The Muses moan:
Thy honey-store
is tearful-dearer
      than our own.

No wasted spring –
Erinna's youth
shall be our wreath
      of song.

from LEONIDAS OF TARENTUM

Before the dawn of your daybreak, man,
time-tallied by sea-sand and *after*
your ghost numbers Time numerous as seed.

Between: a pitiful life; the years,
unsweet, more dwarfish than pin-prick.
Dangling bones – and these are men
on tiptoe to stand as high as clouds
and mocked by a worm at Thread's end,
(O Fates!) nibbling the body's pelt
to less than shreds of leaf . . . to less
than a spider's withered net.

At dawn of every daybreak, O man,
look at your strength; then, lowly as water
flow through scenes that are unadorned. . . .
At dance among the living, in heart
remember how made, and of what straw.

from DIOSCORIDES

Sappho, all-ivied Helicon
and Pieria honor your songs
with those of the Muses.

Raising the pine torch,
Hymen, lord of weddings,
is happy to stand with you
over a bride's flowery bed.

Or you go with wailing Aphrodite
to lament the fair son of Cinyras –
now in the grove of the Blest.

The young love you.
In your dazzling words live
the girls of a deathless mind.

from NOSSIS

O stranger if your stare
goes all the way to Mytilene
adorned of the fair

dances (and they the flames
that kindled Sappho's fiery graces),
remember my times;

let the name of Nossis
be to your sail
as a wind that blesses.

Locris begot my life and death
but the poems sistered me
into eternal youth.

from THE PROCESS

THE HAUNTING

Old walls of brick enriched by changing weather
Stand wide or tall or peaked. Street after street
Has one or two mansions like these, holding the heat
Of hundreds of sunny hours, letting moss gather
Between the crumblings red as flamingo feather.
Or faded to the tints of ripening wheat.
I have passed by these houses in retreat
And felt the known yield power to another,
And heard the voices of another day
Sob through the chinks, and softlier than breath
Descending steps were on the ruined stair
And fingers, vague as cloud, smoothed bricks of clay
And painted cornices.   While underneath
The brightness a dreadful quiet shook the air.

UNPETALED AND UNPEARLED

In chill ecstasy remember
that no one sees; know in somber
pleasure it is by mirrors we look
at the world we unmake.

A periled world in glass...
glassily the figures pass
among machines, and drive machines,
and wince – the sound of breaking means

predicted desolation, yes,
the leveled bridge and villages,
but also a hag-moon terror
revived by a breaking mirror.

Has anyone ever looked with eyes,
seen the Emperor's no-clothes?
My friends stare mirror-distances
as far as the dove-held trees

sounding a deceiving news
either road they choose.
(Glass hearts, be careful what you love,
and careful how you grieve –

or risk a smashing of the bright!
And any savior comes too late!)
Unpetaled and unpearled,
in a glass darkly our wept world.

THE HONEY-EATER

I'm gay in a doom of riddles.
I share the common wound.
The tears upon my hand
Fall from the eating things.
It's the killed linnet sings.

Gone (with it, a sick thinking)
A crush-all winter kinking
The heart, squeezing stone walls.
An end to take-all
Disasters of the will.

Joy is first from food.
The dark sugars rich the blood.
We eat weeping Adonis
(Ourself the sacrifice)
In each holy slice.

The silk slivers, tiny fish
Eaten, juice and flesh,
Consume to the marrow the large.
It is the eater weeps
In the mashed apple pips.

Do the enlightened feed on grief,
Unbelief, as beetles on leaf?
Does the calf treasure the meadow
He gleans to the mustard borders
Crammed with little murders?

I've said it twice and once:
A sour commonsense
Cringes to Epicurus.
Inner sight healing the blind.
The best eating's in the mind.

THE READING

(Theodore Roethke, 1908-1963)

A giant glares, pages loved before
put on a mask.   Choked, famished vines.
The Real slams shut another door.

Beyond the so-called Real, the pain.
This Orpheus also looked back, and so
a delicate dancing of a crane.

Who is Eurydice but the soul
not led from hell but created there,
else she was never kissed at all?

Poems are recited by a rogue
who winks and curses, lolls as he stands
and murmurs, "Roethke, O you dog!"

then, dregs of self, collapsed into a chair,
deaf to gratitude, blind to our love,
gulps cheap sauterne like needed air.

We feed on him. Our joy is a rose
accidentally in his fingers –
he retreats into the hell he knows,

a lizard-leap in "My secrets cry aloud."
Martyr of Apollo and fixed
to the loneliest road.

To the flute, dance his poems. A dawn
too bright sees his "lips pressed upon stone,"
bringing forth the Flower within.

FLOOD

Through all windows and where a door was
the river comes in. Whoever is
overturned by the smell of marsh grass
and heron cries, I like it, I like it!
To help the river over chair and table,
give it the best bed, and see in fireflies
the lamps I paid for, is easy as milk.

Roofs crumble, cows drown in the tree-snags,
and the wired towns yell and flame into char –
that troubles my joy. The streets had been straight
and dry so long! From a drought older and longer,
my stems in a well, my buds beginning,
I ask place and people to breathe and forgive
a river that had no choice but to flow.

A BOY DOWNRIVER

Along the river a boy runs
zigzag from the morning-bell: a dance
of bare feet slamming like books clapped shut;
a point-to-point hopping on flinty stones.

Stabbed by a thorn, nettleburned, an animal
enjoying his muscles in the kill
of a snake. Finding in limestone cracks
pasqueflowers he drinks from a purple bowl.

The fun of being fish, clothes wet
to the bone! Away from the shiny bait
of honors in school (I, I am river)
he lunges at berries, he breathes light,

dazed into torment and joy throwing
sticks at frogs, crushing the pungent snow-
yarrow and shouting dirty words –
a fertility rite his nerves know.

Twilight. Hungry, young, afraid,
he returns to a world he senses is mad –
not really afraid but wishing for supper
and the silent warm meadow of bed.

A boy. A seed of wild power. How long
for a sequoia to grow tall; among
bronzed cattails for a hid cygnet
till the countable stars feather his wing?

A VISITING POET

(for Denise Levertov)

Overlay the streets laid on quick-
sand   arrange them   the dunes of a
child in March   A poppied light: silk,

salt, burnt orange: guarding her feet
from dishonor: freeway debris
winebottle splinter   raw stain

on the sidewalk   Look   (instead
of burning)   The gods come to supper
homemade bread   wine spilled on the robe

Denise   admiring the bal-
let of elderly couples (*"sometimes
the man supports the woman*

*sometimes the woman supports the
man"*) drunkfalling on Pike Street:
lighted up the observations of

the artist: no patching   no fakery
Natural as the northern water-
thrushes: tiny, cinnamonbacked:

wings slyly folded: toeing
through the crowded pungent stems
of herbs to my foot
                    When I look lightly

44

ROCK ELEGY FOR JIMI HENDRIX
(to Lois Parker)

Ow!   the voodoo in your name
turning us on
"third stone from the sun"

Through the black vines of hair & skin
peers the artist, world's dropout

Soul-brothers whatever our myth or color
flower-children clapping & crowding
to touch you, a sacrament

your sound gave us blood-transfusions
when we lay dying as predicted
by computers

The young ones don't jive
they sift your ashes in records & tapes
for the living scream and shout

There is *duende,* as the Spanish
say of genius, in your name
like Wow!   the biggest light

Awfully dark now

THE GHOST OF MY LAI

The girl in the ditch
with her body
is turning bullets away
from baby and grandfather

then her dying scream

witnesses at the trial
say I can't sleep for remembering

the top brass insist
it was a necessary plan

slow slow tree-dancer
in a Noh play
her ghost has power

at her murmur in the dew
o small o fragile my little child
rockbones of moon and earth
clack in deathquake

HILL 882   VIETNAM

When a swallow strangles on a telephone wire
and fallen glass bones and skillful feathers crush
to a flat leaf under a truck, and a paratrooper

branching his green clothes on Hill 882
screaming my god my god: and young blood
leaping from the shattered mouth ends

his breath in a clump of bamboo roots,
agony boils over like milk in a pan
smoking up a stench only the gods enjoy.

I don't save either bird or boy or myself
with a kiss, a word – and going to jail. The morning
star burns me from my pillow, forbidding sleep.

Helpless to wake up the Controllers, nightmare riders
"who make decisions that cost lives," I breathe dust,
the victims whisper the dust into wakefulness.

VIETNAM POSTSCRIPT

Brushing off confetti
of signed petitions

I kneel in a church
Body flown

over the gray
glittering ocean

A boy beginning
as sparrow eggs do

A mother
a profile from Egypt

How can I mourn
as a stone that is mourning?

Will no one scream
and plunge fists at evil?

Hiding this helpless boy
away from the light

"with full military honors"
pretend nothing

It's not your blood
dries in the shadows

WHITE ON BLACK

Into black neighborhood
come chicanos dakota indians
chinese white devils like me
all hungry

From feeling comes sight:
every race flowers   Hear
the victims surviving
in the linnet delirium
singing to the next

Will this be our nest?
black be kind
to brown to yellow
I protest-marched for you
got pneumonia in the icy wind

Endured a murder
Evamay   black sparrow
no gambler   no adulteress
her husband our friend
slit her throat Valentine's Day
hall & steps splashed red
We heard her death scream
tiptoed for days between her drying blood

A black child knocks
don't want cookies   want to talk
with your husband
we ain't got no husband

HAWTHORN

The top beside the head
of a vertical cement stair
a hawthorn tree
patiently   is gathering strength
for the jump.

In the prolonged wet & cold
a tree has difficulties;
traffic-vapor coats the buds,
the roots agitate
                    a rotting water.

A jump into what?
The necessity
to make seed is patient,
a repeated tug.

Small birds
quick as raindrops
skip on the greening sticks.

Getting oily pollen
on their feet,
knocking off petals
scented, oval, glistening.

The tree
fills   with a huge breath;
gets on with its work.

THE KITCHEN WINDOW

Roots are squeezed by a box
set in pavement; air is kept from the deeper
roots; poisoned air
and gray light remain to the gasping leaves.

An overcoming of horror,
the tree looks into a timidly-high
town horizon
                    at the moon
plated with marble.
By day a ghost of cloud, an isolated
                    water lily
the new office building
swimming in blue unbreathable carbons –
                    the constant moon.

Full, any night,
let the windows be crescent or gibbous
as late workers and cleanup crews
slacken, gulp coffee.

The limited joy in a jail
shapes the exchange
between tree and a marble
moon.
            The force fleshing a stone
and the bones, in approval
quakes the wide glass,
whips the soiled branches.

THE PROCESS

I do hear or maybe I feel the bounce
the creak the ring of stress, wood
on metal, the building torn from its roots,
glass fighting the windowframes. Rain digs
into pavement and distant foothills, raindrops
pummel and jump; then the dense clouds
crumble under the weight of the sun;
the roar between raindrops is a war of tribes.

Like that pigeon shaking off storm outside
the cracked window I feel or I hear the sun
as delight, I catch glints of a wisdom before
it is lost in the big and right brightness:
*What is the mind that its pleasure is a rock
anchoring a wave* even as water overturns
quiet and grains in the rock are always spinning?

THE BED

At the door of a cluster
of apartments
early sun rouges the parts
of an unexpected flower
as I look at chrome and
shiny cloth a cool turquoise:
delivery of a new bed
by two men in decent black.

Then the neighborhood-faces
brown, white, dark,
portraits on stamps stuck to windows,
hover in the tense quiet.

The men return,
neither sparrow nor dogbark
accompanies the unfolded bed.
The black coats lifting the huddle
under gay blue blankets
stumble at the bottom of the stairs.

He refuses a sip of my coffee,
the dead are a peculiar nation,
he rents his solitude elsewhere.

from DARK TO GLOW

SURVIVOR

All of his banners
shot down
the last silk threads
carried off
by the ragpickers

He tells the nurse
sponging his weariness
so much left to do

Under the clean shirt
and underpants
the skinny flesh
the inexorable bones

refusing to die

Death will know
he's been in a fight
when the cornfield is seeded

THE LEAVING

His reservation is beyond
conducted tours to Scandinavia.
A bad time for a trip:
tornado, phone wires down,
boats sinking.

Bringing *bon voyage,*
careful of new shoes,
I tiptoe through mud & cinders

Cars trucks buses
an attack of tigers.
I wave my mouth:
Don't hit this messenger.

I open a shopping bag
for his glazing eyes.
Choose: fruit or yogurt.

He doesn't know me
thinned by traveling
his time and mine.
Or remember our coupling
that shook the thrones
of stellar power.

MEMORIAL (I)

Pillowed, a noble painted by Velasquez;
he has dominated all crises to reach
his particular goal – as I smooth
clammy arms, hear the rattle in throat,
wipe the death-dew from the brow of my lover.
"Can you hear me? I said your special word."
Lucid eyes open, a radiant smile
for my touch and a last, last Yes.

FOR PAUL

I make no moan or outcry, just don't sleep.
The rain staining, etching the windowpane,
takes care of tears. Awake without hope
he will drink the morning with me, intone
a comment to my rhyme. What a lot of breath
went into the loving and now it's dying
we have to think of. The ghost on his path —
I refuse to believe what it is saying,

recalling the heron-river, books read aloud,
the nights we talked, sending the moon away.
The weedy places we rolled in and hid,
each to the other changing dark to glow.
You cannot lose me, said his ringing Yes
between the death-sweat and my forlorn kiss.

SECOND WIFE

Slowly he accepts ice cream...
between the half-teaspoons
I feed him
he talks of Daisy,
grammar school idol;
repeats the story
of his first wife Minna.

He has used up more life
than I can imagine: at sixteen
goldmined in Alaska, killed a thief
trying for his poke.

Ranched in Leavenworth,
befriended Indians
against his neighbors;
sold strawberries
to the railroad women. Lectured
on mind-enchantment to movie starlets,
was paid top prices for mystery stories.

I listen to his tales, a Desdemona
pitying, unbelieving – not really enraged
at the waste of my youth.

I burn in the flame of his cremation.
Sorting my ashes from his I wonder
what will I remember at my end:
not the boys I danced with,
not even the delight of his mind.
Surely a tree in the alley
lighted by a finch singing louder
than the din of ash-cans.

MEMORIAL (II)

The blackcopper cat has given up hope,
no longer sits on his bed refusing to eat
until his return. She leaps on my slacks,
kneads the cloth, nests there. The feline heat
warms me from the chill of loss. Is she
a medium aware of future dimensions?
Paws quiver, shaking off river sand,
treading in the footprints of the dead.

ELEGY BY MOONLIGHT

This is too bright a landscape for the grief
come to being with the first white rose,
sleeping and waking with me when summer leaf
hid redbirds and their songs. Now autumn sows
seeds of sleep that will not grow in me;
forgetting – a slow drug wearing away.
You who are blown deathward out to sea,
even my grief is mottled with decay.

In twigtipped glimmering a blond moon rolls,
might be a spider strengthened by the pang,
webbing her hunger on black roughened poles;
might be your laugh. The cry burns on my tongue:
You seem forever lost in solitude.
All but the memory weaving in my blood.

THE PROMISE

What pulled me from the re-dreaming
of love's wild times is the echo of my voice:
Why are you here, you're dead!
Glad to see you of course,
changed to the photos of young manhood.

We never quarreled about money
yet he talks about dividing
seashells, feathers, flowerheads,
in the bank account;
he to go his way, I going mine.
One way of leaving the delight-grief
of a life.

His blindness! a car could hit him.
That was a bad dream, he says, laughing
unquenchable. Where he is, multi-sight
like a spider's eye, he sees deep.

My stone-heart cracks at the hint
of the message: he lives, he loves
enough to endure return to tell me.

from MIDSUMMER RITES

SUN AND AMIABLE AIR

Sun and amiable air
Suddenly, where had been
Cloud everywhere; and within
Cloud and cold a door
Opens: other callings to hear.

You've been washing the dark
Things of thought all the night
Of a lightless season; delight
Yourself in the white work
Finished, brighter than white.

Grass, the smallest petals
Yellow and underfoot blue
Are a speech of rattles
And cymbals breaking through
The washed globe to tell you –

To tell you to be their voice
Rejoicing that the nights end.
On the songs of willow wand
The wren-wing mornings rise,
The sorrow-washed hearts ascend.

GOING BY JET

How deep is high thirty-seven-thou-
sand feet. Under the cobbled cloud
towns flatten, a striped land folds and weaves.
Sun reaches me. Not as it happened
to Icarus, drowned pioneer.
I could trample it like daisies.

But my heart knocks in the abyss
of air. Not with fear. The metal pod
contains from danger its temporary seeds.
With desire. Comes the hope of this flight
the long looped birdclouded river,
lost as soon as looked at. My mind
hugs water, will take home the muddy smell
of an earth pulled up with the grass.

ONE MEMORY OF ROSE

A young, vexed, and desired woman
her skin like a calla lily,
she is our mother
homesick for birch land,
in a city flat
beat us and threw on the floor
the breakfast she had cooked.

Sun brightens the roof tiles,
the ocean enters with the air –
but I had to be her mother
and theirs:
I picked up the brown-paper lunches,
whispered fierce comfort,
and to my chilled knees
and cotton skirt
gathered the younger girl
and the little boy.
On the way to school
this group hesitating at the door.

Kiss me, said the Maenad tearing at her head,
a fear and a disdain of earthly chances
glaring her sea-purpled eyes,
you'll never see me again.
A daily ritual.
Always we kissed her.

THE FOUR O'CLOCKS

A scent stings my breath, stops the laughing
in summer with my children and husband.
They wonder at my tears, that I pull
the coarse leaves, magenta blooms, for a bouquet –
imitating a Friday buried below memory.

An old-country custom is to give the newborn
the name of a relative newly-dead – drops of wine
to soothe the unhoused spirit.
My mother exhausted from giving life
moans in her blueblack hair at the passing of Tante Sylvie,
and my half-gypsy father has to consent.

Not in his dreams: He had promised the dying woman,
Laika from his horsetrading province, the name;
groans in the sheets when my fulfilled mother demands
"Do you need the priest – or a doctor?" He has seen night
after night Laika in her graveclothes reproaching him . . .
Does a Rom cheat his own? . . . and visits the graveyard.

I remember Laika, yellow-white hair braided
around a smile, voice like the windstirred birches.
She used to send me to buy Turkish cigarets,
the street air was hot and flavored with cinnamon.
And little Sylvie. Four months are too short for a life
but not for love. The flowers I picked were her last bouquet,
I would not, I would not go to the funeral.
I sat among the ice melting from her heated flesh
and dumped on the sunburnt lawn.

Did the dead woman's anger poison the child?
A problem for churchmen. She withered in summer fires
like this grass and that herb, trailing aromas
freshening a dried-up grief. Alerted to the children's
sober looks I promise honey to spread
on buns. Giving the honeycomb to my husband
who will break it into unequal pieces.

THE WAITRESS

She comes with Greek coffee, lazuli sky, lazuli sea,
sun-whitened walls of her town. My book is open
to the next assignment, Plato. She translates into
the vernacular, gently corrects my stammering
syntax. In the afternoon lull she leans on my table,
dark hair, lemon skin glimmer. Come to Lindos,
Next Year in Lindos, the recurrent dream. Grapes
cooling in the well, after harvest the feasting, the
singing around a fire on the beach. I am too shy
to tell her that some desires are born with broken wings.

Living and dying in a tall city she makes me a song:
I'll give you a donkey ride to top of the mountain;
wine scented with basil flowers – when the guns
are dead, the knives rust, when man's heart opens like
woman, like a child, to the compassion of the dust.

BY ANOTHER ROAD

Where has the voyaging
through nights of days and days
taken me to what rock I cling?

(Whatever uses me
for cave, womb, grave,
is skillful in mockery.)

Consider the cities I spilled
as carelessly as milk,
and the handful of sand I held;

consider the vision I had;
the Hero walking on water,
lover, loving, and the love of God.

Whitehanded love, fivepointed surprise,
an acid sweetness of white flowers,
it unlocked a house

curtained with starry tricks.
And I jigged there, I shouted
my game of embers and sticks –

till I rushed aflame, my hair
and my bones, and the house
and the universe burned bare.

Sift the ashes, a seed
survives, the fruit was sturdy;
more life, by another road.

HOMAGE TO PLOTINUS

You *inward* man godward gazing
while writing, talking to friends
or resting (hearing a rainless fishflight)
from your asphodel, change me.

Refloat my in-sunk cargo – it was my guilt
wrecked the thrushes in a sweetened space.
The lilies I broke, the starry lilies
gathered and forgotten; the anise-steeped
music seized and forgotten, refloat in me.

Among the lank, leaf-rattling stems I learned
a child's red-apple language, spelling like a child.
I bit winetawny pears, the juice was sticky
with the names you left, names canceling all names.
I sang them on my fingers, of them I made
an iron rope to moor the rock-wrecked heart.

Was it a wreck? The rocks, dry, white, and hot;
the cereals, burned to white, trodden straw;
air, ocean, villages roll in the rocking light –
most dazzling when the mind has quenched all light
even its own, waving it bright good-by.

I tell no lie in telling nothing of time.
A mountain range of minutes, the dried blood aching.
I do dive deep, rise high, release arrow
completely to the target. *Plotinus.* A thought
snaps me into your mind of asphodel.

You are my father more surely than the sperm –
it kindled me to grieve in a fevered body;
you coax me into knowing most lightfulness
springs from the lonely names of the Alone.
Do you send me back? To a chaos of sharks and men?
I do return and tell those lawless angels
they are marble, they *dream* their lunges of murder –
chaos is the dance of *order in transition*.

MIDSUMMER RITES

Amen! counts the ship's clock: six bells
recording men far from their beginnings tumbled
in a hallway drunken sleep; the wives of fishermen
and airpilots turning without ease, dreaming the lost signals.
Three o'clock in the morning: O when I danced
dancing to excited trumpets or fierce joy, boys in Vietnam
whirled from the deathly dark into incessant light
have danced away the last night of their blood.

I am wideawake – *did you ever sleep*
mocked my tornup heart – *did you hallucinate*
when obedience to love was all your care?
The linden tree on a street jackhammer-splintered
is leafing, soon will be honeybudded and yellow
with butterflies, a fulfilled self rooted in a world
not ours, unaware of the graceless hunger, loneliness.

In midsummer light I anatomize the concrete
of love: its divisions the facets of an heirloom jewel.
The earliest gleam was my grandmother, prudent, cynical,
whose small fat hands clapping at my voiced despairs
nestled me, words, young bones, into her eiderdown.
Then a boy in a silvered wild-oat time, reading Keats
to a wondering child; and where-when came the Shakespeare
wisdom and song to be my pillow, *mandragora*
from the street-hard green-wild sleepless nights?

Love of another kind stung membrane and vein
into melody, a poignant gaiety like Mozart;
the dazzled sperm and ovum swimming close

in the milky ocean of his sounding stars.
Unripe I loved. Hoping to escape the ordained loneliness.
And missed my chance. Fell from the bird-theurgic element
an unblued jay, a tuneless finch, scratching with blunted claws
the dirtied names of love on a public wall.

In a garden, mindless as a leaf, fingers deep into soil,
staring at cloud images in a raindrop,
ritually waving the lamps of fireflies;
is it for love of an astral dream the warmongers,
treekillers, are sowing the earth with fiery salt –
nothing shall stand but their perverse temple?

Midsummer moon slaps alive a new baby to its name
of hero or victim – it must choose. All that blood.
Be a rock in a river – no escape. The rock exists
entranced by agony, the Love-creative in all its grains,
a Shadow whipping the shadows of ourselves.
Amen! counts the ship's clock crazed by the dawning light
ringing 2-4-6-8 bells at once. *Praise love! Praise love!*

PART II

UNCOLLECTED POEMS

COVER OUR LOVE

Moon coming great
through gloom of the trees,
wind that has died
to the lisp of a breeze:

cover our love
lest it be seen,
lest shadow of light
come between.

Let us be hidden,
worn with delight,
in the kind covers
of cool lingering night.

If he should waken
with day in the sea,
his bright naked flesh
would prevail over me.

Moon coming great –
he sleeps   and the kiss
curves on his mouth
as my breast curves to his.

KINGS FOR LOVE

Are we lovers? Nights of a shared bed,
And all the separate voyages of dreaming.
I am not skilled in dreams; a plum's my need,
A book, a fence, a river on my hand,
A revel at table, and the rowdy voices.
But the wish of my mind is not my friend.

I sleep·sound and long, not *his* unwilling sleep.
He found a well, he talks with the Keeper of Wells.
He returns, wet as the newborn, having dived deep.
He loves me. A fact not to be questioned. That shines
Like a house of gold in a mist of flowers.
Yet we are strangers and we follow different signs.

Self-love tells me to copy him, to go
(Fearless or fearing but go) and to that point
Inside the zero: *to be nothing is to know:*
(Not as the dead know – meek, learning by rote
The riddling truths, myths, legends of the grave)
Breathing and choosing in the jeweled world.
Forsaking kingdoms. Becoming kings for love.

Stars dropped these thoughts into my eyes, like dew.
Audible azure, a jay's receding carillon,
Sleep is torn, our drowsy fingers tear it
(O gilded light!) to let the three notes through.

NIGHT WALK

Lamps of the warehouse city turned down,
    only a bridge chain glimmering over
    cobalt bend and ice-flecked river
    hints outline of the dulling town.
Daring the streets where no lamps shine
    I glow to Orion's shoulder-quiver,
    and the belted three stars cover
    headlands blurred with oak and pine.

I don't turn sleepers from the dream
    their furious desires are weaving.
What if I roused them to the clap
    of towered stars, voices joined to flame?
Without landmarks of their own believing
    they would be lost, the way so steep.

NIGHT WORKERS LEAVE AT DAWN

Leaving mills that house
A nightmare boulevard,
A lint-and-resin river,
They behold a sky in rose.

Within, a risen day
And dusty noon; night, never.
They wince in electric suns,
Acid smells, engined bray.

But this summered morning watch
That bird among twigs
Prickly with swelled bud, how new
And silk he is to touch!

So young, he feels no omen-grief,
Feather-loss, hawk-talon terror;
A new reader of the riddle
Of being – his beginning, safe.

Never number this day among losses.
Less hopelessly they hear a newcomer
Recite the riddle-terms
Above the moving grasses.

He flies on a screech of sorrow.
Work continues from dark to dark;
The riddle remains; the darkened men
Reserve its reading for tomorrow.

IN BACKYARDS HALFWAY PINK

In May
the town smells like a tea-chest:
tiny blooms
engage the wind, insects,
to set berry, apple, peach.
Unperceived by the boys
snapping off branches.

A carpenter
stares beyond the little boys
handing him nails
through gilt threads of rain
tethering his senses.

Does he glimpse
other loves and roads?

The man is made of earth
and bits of sky.
He gives to his boys
in the pink-honeysuckle wet
shrilly imploring
the use of the hammer.

TREE SEEDS

Over highrise office & condominium persistent
the annual crow scratches air for a tree.
Which one the nest?

Cones of the white pine open like thighs
after love, a wind catches the kernels.

Willow has a different wing.
Among tufts like ephemeral thistle.

Wet in a stream or buried by squirrels
the black walnut pierces its sculptured husk.

Hazel shades the salmon in a pool,
cracks pod, shoots into the future.

Fifty years till an oak make seed.
The seed enduring perils of the astronaut.

Crow's choice is a fir
in a tattered playground.

REDTAILED HAWK

The several visits to the Turkey Timber farm
he learned new skills: could plow a straight row
with mules, then the tractor. Milked 15 Guernseys,
one, Daisy, would not let anyone else milk her
till she felt he was gone. Continued to play
with the friend's nephews, pick strawberries
for a favorite dessert; he was getting taller,
itching from a loneliness he had no name for.

Stole her out of a tall-pine nest
(leaving two noisy beaks) to be his kin.
Reckless of parent wings returning to mash
young bones to the furrow. The redtail taloned
his shoulder, morning-evening chores, the clean manure
smell, the chickens clucking, a shared world. Peering
into his eyes to know his mind. Yellow satin breast,
autumnleaf on back, a stare like the aggies he rolled.

Back to town and school. His little sister hunted
and tossed grasshoppers to the quick pounce, the big house
was free to growing wings; evenings they played – bird
and boy – reliving hawk-stoop and rise with the catch.

When an oakleaf's the size of a gopher's ear
it's cornplanting time, mating-nesting time,
the redbrick house is a cage. He took her to the woods.
She flew to the tops, looked around, came back to his shoulder.
Her grieving whistle must have broken windowglass
miles away. In the freedom of trees she will forget
her first lover – gulping tears, hobbled to the earth.

PRINCESS MAQUOKETA

Dead so long, the young warrior who loved true
Also dead, you live in a truant's wonder:
Skipping stones into a river named for you,
The pebbles hurt, my bare feet stung by cinder,
I wade for healing of my too-late love.
The water lilies spread whiter than feather,
Some oaks you knew remain a native grove
Bright as your doeskin in the Indian weather.

Punished for leaving school I lie in bed
Imagining your beauty: it is not flesh
To crumble and decay – not in my head.
Young as I am I know that skull or ash
Has no traffic with you: The river says
The same and – noisy in a wind – the trees.

THE ANTIDOTE

Extreme old age secretes a liquid
that maddens. Yet my great-uncle,
a cat with more than nine chances,
feeds his dyed-black moustache, touches
a gold earring for luck, revising
his memoirs to include a celebrated *geisha*.
Her rice paper portrait is on the wall.

The times he is penniless he will not visit
our table; nibbles at dusk his cakecrumb memories:
drinks to a cloud white as the mountain.
Winning at the races smiling he appears
with a load of gifts and festival winks.

In dance to his whistling
"I wonder who's kissing her now"
I demand more words. All left to him
is "buying the wine." Writing all night,
ruined eyes, he shines a message:
Don't cross your fingers
in the habit of living.

TALL LITTLE BROTHER

In the supermarket peaches are big, bright,
and without scent. I eat them in memory:

Running through the warm Vallejo midnight.
Calling a neighbor already changing flannel
nightgown for professional dress. Flinging through
beaded portieres to rouse the navy doctor.
Promising the dark orchard at the corner
– mossgreen peaches, bloodjuice in the pulp –
this small girl will take care of the child.

When our mother worn out with the crying
of a sick baby threw him into my bed
I caught the bundle and rocked it quiet.
All through childhood I took him with me,
even to Charlie Chaplin movies.
Carried him pick-a-back to the playground.

He was accident-prone: at two broke his arm
falling to the sidewalk; at sixteen,
mangled in a truck mix-up. Once, he lost an eye.
Other years my letters tried to save him
thousands of miles away.

A note from his widow after the funeral:
victim of the freeway.

He was deft with words, affable – unlike our father –
till I beat them both at cardgames.
Eyebrows quivered with rage.
I have outlived the role of sister-mother.
Rotting peaches in the cold midnight.

ONE MEMORY OF FRISCO

My father had several trades, none of them really
suited to a country town; he was a carnival man
in a business suit. His poetry was cards, the kings
and aces liked him; sometimes he won a team or the surplus
of a shop and dreamed of power. Anyhow from them he got
a respectable living. Once in his lazy way he found himself
in Mexico, bid on the melon fields in flower – against the advice
of his gesticulating *amigos,* who knew the ropes.
His gamble made a fortune; we, his children, wore velvet and gold
chains; dancing, crushed poker chips into the carpet – till the horse
accident. Three months in hospital and a butcher who thought
      he was
a surgeon – *You can't win them all,* said my frivolous father.

Limping into the city, holding me by the hand,
he rides the ceremonial elevators to offices and penthouse
of managers and presidents; all doors wide to his presence.
A bulky man smelling of cigars gives me a box of Dolly Varden
chocolates – one of the heroines of my mother's Dickens reading –
and tells me to go play. Cream and fruit centers loll on my tongue.
I spit out the licorice bits, dribbling black syrup on my tattered
      lace vest and cuffs.
In a dreamy munching, I hear laughter from my father's fairytales,
condolence he will never dance again, and clink of gold coins.

One must speak well of the dead. I admired his courage in defying,
over the years, my slim mother's true-steel will. And besides,
this memory is sweetened by the best chocolates.
With the unwisdom of a woman-child I thought
what is he that these men like him so much? Now I understand:
no clown but *Pan,* no liar but the truth of springtime.
His hazel eyes and handsome moustache glistening with brandy
tolerantly he slaps my questions: Goose, what can a lame man do
till he is healed – if ever? I am selling lottery tickets.

HALLUCINATEDWHEELCHAIR

It's a small town, the nursing home:
friendly calls, chair to chair;
whispering gossip about the staff.

Gladys is the odd element,
gray eyes sparkling with unreason –
stamping black boots, smoking a man's pipe,
loosing a warrior's yell.

She recognizes me by the cigaret
I light to keep her company;
some days she sticks pigeon feathers
into her headband. *Pocahontas* I cry,
her answering gobble is sane
and the offer of pipe.

Then the chair whirls
through Ozark blackberries,
climbs the white of Alps;
she flies, flies – a tree goddess.

Travel-wearied by mind's tornado
I touch the braided knots of white hair,
she laughs gibberish at the ghost
pointing her to the Navajo Trail.

THE HOSTAGE

Neither inn nor prison the three-tiered cube of wood
soot-and-snowstained, has a military look,
like Castle Pomfret a place for hostages.

He lies in a bed by the window, watching
the spin of king's-yellow leaves. Invisible points
of an invisible crown pierce to the bone.

There are weeks he pretends he is not king,
talks very fast, is always running, comes
to our picnics, or eats alone in the park.

More times he lies in that room at the top of the house,
talking to the moon – a Carmelite nun
or a nurse – lamenting the pointed crown.

He complains although a servant he has bribed
would wear it for him it will not come off!
And, Death, he is sure, that obsequious skull,

will be polite – and incompetent. Then a wind
rises, the boughs droop saffron in the morning light.
Then he sleeps a little behind his staring eyes.

ELEGY: e.e.cummings

Now the moon is a dimmed eye.
Why should it trouble the moon
that a skylark left our sky?

A season of butterfly,
equinox, I write again –
to be read by the dimmed eye:

"No flute more sweetly a cry
than your winged words had shine,
larking and leaving our sky."

Beautiful with rage; not shy
with angels; he went like rain
clouding a moon of dimmed eye.

The most alive had to die!
I break my heart on that stone,
cry: *"O lark shaken from sky!"*

Let the moon be a dimmed eye,
he remains in our love by
words that keep the summers green.
A skylark in poem of sky.

A FILM REVIVAL

Sun's flesh lighting up flowers, that's
what she was. Honeycomb we ate
like the chapters of St. John;

        brighter we hurled. Traffic light
        changing, wait! To her pang a dim
        doctor stooped a dark goblet.

I am begging for Marilyn
(dove of Aphrodite) Monroe.
Clutch my fingers, a god will hear.

        A man falls: came out of a shop
        and fell down, light knocking him wide.
        "Don't touch me!" screaming at my hand.

The green light jumping
a man glares, gets up to hell
his own way. *Weep but for*

        joy, little sister: set
        as a seal upon love, on love's
        mouth as a sunflower poem.

BACH CONCERT

The polite hall is wreathed
with Della Robbia
porcelain emitting fragrance.

I look at the incoming musicians,
some are girls in long flowery dresses,
close my eyes to hear the tones
sliding into meditation for a friend
newly dead . . . how can I help her struggle
yellow-black-striped caterpillar
into butterfly?

The music stings my eyelids. I begin
a litany: *dwell perfect   be perfect
wherever you are.* My companion swims
in the tense sound, he does not observe
what is happening to my hands
resting on the program: they have risen
6 inches. Scared, I close my eyes tight,
listening to Bach
lifting my hands even higher,
opening an astral window.

A FRIENDLY NIGHT

(to Marguerite Caetani)

Almost no one shakes the night
for the deserted weedy stars
to taste   beyond the junipered
coldfiery stuff in glasses   himself

In a west tree   *Sirius*   cut-diamond
a dolphin sailing a wave and spray
the wished night in my skull buried
teak tongue clappering gayest lies

to my mind walking suburban blocks policed
by billboards and where trees are springing willow
from the mill-smoke river   our voices
laugh/clash   the gin rocking up a storm

Rushing their bar-shiny cars the uncelibate
adore a jukebox dusk   my charity flows
to the beat   what I need and need no one brings
bringing often a filled full wet-stemmed glass

Four of us   all mask removed   friendly
we sit   the square of form   the universe
Not completely deaf to the wrecking hammer
drum enchantment   to our lovely night

MOMENT IN MUSEUM

A teasing woman, a stone head glowing down,
Returning my look with almost living wonder,
Tells me a fable more durable than stone.

A marble that was white, white as a bone,
Has yellowed, but the broad eyelid is tender.
A teasing woman, a stone head glowing down.

Mouth of coquette, mild as a quarter moon,
Though she bit down on wisdom's bleakened cinder,
Tells me a fable more durable than stone.

No bigger than a cup, without a crown,
A trifle in the museum's hoard of splendor.
A teasing woman, a stone head glowing down.

That her curls stirred and in a sealight shone
Before there were two thousand years of grandeur,
Tells me a fable more durable than stone.

Lark, hyacinth, and *lover – briefly known*
And greatly loved – these continue to defend her,
A teasing woman, a stone head glowing down
To tell a fable more durable than stone.

VACATION IN ROME

Reading *The Pisan Cantos*
not sleeping much
airborne
the body is stubborn
won't believe any clock
but its own

where am I at 4 a.m.?

On the way to the Coliseum
to get something the Roman gods
saved up for me –
and it didn't get lost
or stolen.

Moss, birds and I
see the rosy-toed dawn
nudge pink, yellow, blue
out of old dry stones.

Wish I had learned
the language of green
then moss would explain
the depth of surprise.

ODYSSEY '69: A Book Review

Merci mille fleurs
for the magic carpet
transports the reader
from Amsterdamish rain-dismal
to "my home   ionian isles"

I dance among the syllables
enlightened by precision
into the marble beauty
the photographs
and dance back
to the holiness of words

"Erosos,
Sappho's birthplace,
is on the western end of Lesbos"
On western sand   in west waters
I walk barefoot: rock and sky
violets and olive trees
remember the Tenth Muse

"The Greeks are light eaters"
Let this book be eaten
lightly
Crumble a leaf of basil
the kingly herb
into the nourishing dish
Smell the white flower of it
as you sip the Homeric wine

RAIN AND HAVEN

To half-lit rooms rented by strangers
I arrive for hiding, here will be hidden
A rainblurred writing and a secret.

My pieces of dropped porcelain
Tied in a grimy rag, rainsoaked,
Dance their cracked colors, wildest light.

Now must the rain of fair speech moisten
The mind's dry acre; let the rain
Sing the praises of lake-seasons.

Might be a deputy of *Landfinder*,
Restorer-of-bread, allows me roof
And a chair – rain, sing of him.

Might be for wintered *Sirius*
His secret agents, strangers take me in.
Sing, little words, resembling rain.

All of the haunted are havened ... somewhere ...
By omen, knocking; and answered like me
For my pages of book, my pieces of vase.

WOODCARVING: OWL FAMILY

(Philip McCracken)

1

Stiller than raceme of plum, clumped like toes,
tight braids, they cling to the owlet.
Teaching stillness as the device of flying.

Within the triangle that art is based on,
the Holy Family of Egypt; extended through madonnas
of the Chair and the Pomegranate.

2

The Wood arrows memories of M'Owl,
orphaned russet, living in one big room,
from him I learn the why of the down-edge wing.
Three days he perched on the tall bookcase,
flapping and flapping a hurricane of feathers.

Then into the heated air a soundless sailing
around and around till I am dizzy; the descent
to my wrist and the triumphant glare eye to eye.

Leisure is mother of the arts; M'Owl seemed to invent games.
A predator, he chose the pickpocket skills;
Lie on the bed, eyes shut, then the tap on hand.
Soundless as his flight, he had removed keys, cards,
from all pockets. Again, tap on hand – *replace them.* The game
is renewed to the gleam in fathomless eye.

3

Mating season, turned free in a river-sanctuary,
he returned twice with a family.
And flew into silence, having learned
all the piercing lessons of stillness.

MOONWORT IN AMHERST

Those grape-cluster circles I keep
all winter: *Lunaria,*
the big book said. *Moonwort.*
Tint of the freeway-cement
after rain under lamplight.

Petals give place to
"three translucent valves"
green and tawny then bruised to purple,
splitting, rolling, dropping beans –
a feather rowing home –
the lasting disk is satin.

A cycle lived by Emily
stitching time into a seamless
shroud. *Honesty,* the plant's
country name, is her bone and word,
her bee-dancing at hive mouth
the distance by sun
                       to unearthly honey.

HOMAGE TO MORRIS GRAVES, PAINTER

I

INNER EYE EAGLE WITH CHALICE

May it be to you standing per-
plexed before his birds the dare –
To know god by his feather

Unknot the habitual,
fallen threads trace "eyeball," "moon-
halo" on the Chalice – myself

in memory resembling the Chalice
From the moonstone an eagle
at the halt between flights, a mind

at dance in talon, tendril
Eyes piercing like mirror-bits
to the bone gash me into

calm of the Inner Eye floating
in bliss beyond greed and pain
Dipping beak into the moon's cup

II
SPIRIT BIRDS

Gleam
            within a bronze ritual bowl
the minnow observes these birds as
infinite strata of consciousness

Circling
            a bough, a wave, a cloud,
with eyes like the Eye in a domed
church ceiling they splinter glass,

sting the light through starry fragments
Other pairs are the Judge, black hat pro-
nouncing Death by Hanging: "Can you

endure the weight of your choices?"
The eye of a minnow held in beak
of a heron is unterrified

The fact
            upbearing the spirit
digs in with sharp toes, strong legs braced
A feather smells like country butter

THE WALL REMEMBERED

is invisible
to bulldozers

unaware of movement
the irregular oblongs
of limestone

cling to each other
without cement

purple tints
in the fossil grain
dented, creviced,

hollowed: wasps, red-eyed
flies, a catalpa sprout,
know the stone is home

and a striped lizard
runs over moss
waving a satinblue tail

EXILE FROM *WHERE*

(*Costmary, camomile, St. John's wort,*
sing the children; the children plait wreaths,
hang over gate their mugwort dolls.)

You, exiled from *where*,
the earth's enchanted flowering
you read as wishes and witchways.

Who slew the ivied ox
to fatten fields, brought the goat-
sacrifice to drench vines,

from the glass-face, steelhooped
streets to airport (your eyes, *pietà,*
your blood, unceasing Niobe),

you search your hand for scars:
the thorns talking; desert devils,
how they whispered; the dragon-

abysses breathing pitch, and talking.
Longest day looms, costmary yellow.
You, drunken with weeping, slept

centuries; now you call to the
yellow, *O candle, lighted in*
twelve houses guarded by animal

stars, all of earth's new
mullein will not keep the ice-
quench from that flame nor my blood!

You, looking for other-
than-creature, how you sob
in the motored silence,

Father (over fire) *find thy son* –
(the fabled way back to *where!*)

(*Vervain, hawkweed, fern,*
sing the children; the children plait wreaths,
hang over gate their mugwort dolls.)

THE WEB AND THE DROPS
(to Mary Randlett)

Spider, between posts,
loomed a cloth – torn in the wind,
mended by raindrops.

More than wood holds up
the old stairs. The spinner knows
a wisdom of thread.

Strength of a cut tree
serves a man's foot – the web
keeps the sky from falling.

After rain, bare twigs
glimmer with transparent flowers.
Wilting as they bloom.

She runs on uneven
water-shapes – feeling damage,
finds a new world.

As seeds viewed through glass,
insect-eggs enlarged by art,
she sees the raindrops.

Among drops like seals
on a Chinese scroll, the spider
reties her web.

TREES, NEAR AND FAR

Palm and acacia. A new city pinned to parks.
A dragon-writhe in sand is the tea-leaf tree.
I walk and look. No tree, no tree mistressing me.

Of the *where* I've been, where do I want to be?
Another useless thought hung in the mind.

A cloth is given me to make a coat.
A thread appears, I sew with either hand.
I bite the pungent thread of memory:

A far day in dust, moon-shreds wetted with dew,
A moon losing feathers; a spinningwheel bewitched.
Thousands of yards of yarn – wave-white, cloud-blue.

Flying up and down, the elms descending,
Oblique across the black leaves of an elm,
Incarnate thoughts, a thought paired with a bird.
The dark birds falling, black stones into pale foam.

They practiced flight formations,
Growls in the throat, brusque cries and muttered cries.
Downriver they flew; they died; they fly these days.

Of the *where* I've been, *what* do I want to be?

Palm and acacia fade and fill my sight.
Laughing I run, believing elm and birds are there,
Are here. Preening their atoms in breaking light.

BROTHER-BODY, SISTER-MIND

cells   organs   secretions
you invade my country
of meditation

force the virgin
to bleed again
the deluded rapture

FAST HEART the doctor said
are you trying   to kill me
for loving the mind?

A pot of *Triteleia coerulea*
blossoms on the fire-escape
white petals ribbed with blue

the fragrance rides me
to Africa, the exulting mind
urging more life

let death have his joke.

HIEROGRAM OF ORDER

Smoke (that streaks dingy the cotton river)
Darkens the dark-red brick, drags into night
A yellowing crag.

And factory-dinge shakes out the blue plumes
Of *Kneph:* Nile-fire, of *Osiris* the other face,
Arranging chips of chaos to a velvet of order.

His bridges swing
In a fishwind threshing the islands.
Gay Daemon, O hammered world scented with sawdust,
He flows hot in our copper, the air-drills dance.

But the Orphic egg is crushed.
But the rocket-missiles hawk any city.

Under a highway tarmac
Grain-seed, tree-seed moaning.
Death of a hill, the unborn of birds keening.
A mile of streets
The mechanical jaws chewing and spitting,
The pieces of houses moan.

The dream-weepers fall
Through an ice of cities; a freezing dark
Of blighted field. Read them awake

With the shout carved on the rock-paws of the Sphinx:

Kneph *brings down the fat from their high places,*
He collects the cracked stones.
He makes stones into men by a nod of His plume.

THE MAKER OF APRILS

The masses of my fellows uncreate
in one week the millioned-year
Creation: the Furies lead the great
unmaking, their torches everywhere.

That is the devil-mask of things
frightening the luckless to their graves.
April's green folk of former springs
set up by tribes their tents of leaves.

The Maker of April tunes the stars,
their golden music sprinkles bloom:
Violets are purple as the pairs
of starlings, lilies like shells or foam.

The delighted Maker comes to no end
of making, be it moth or spire
in marble, be it the beginning fire
of a heart toward the fathering Friend.

HISTORICAL

The battle-names in stone, the fire-marred flags
will testify it was historical,
this time we live in, simple to our breathing
as a distant hill dug out of blue,
as the odor of noon in sun-spread hair.

It is the jump of light on working chimneys
flowered and tasseled like apple trees and corn.
It is May surprising us with white cathedrals:
bells shake girls out of bed and into veils.

Scholars will say, "An age heraldic with broken towns
and counting by years of famine..." but we have it
as a listening to laughter under streetlamps.
Boys forget the scorching guns they carried,
to look at summer, and love begins   begins again.

BLUES FOR PAUL

face down
crossed sticks
flung
at a bed

my man
acts out disaster

don't scream
nobody heard
the three-month innocent
smothered in crib
the napalm burns
on village bodies

don't believe
you slut   you ruined me

slice onions   carrots
for a stew
food is a healing

my man and I
knifing each other
continue to dance

goddamsonofabitch

gnaws out of my throat
that impolite word
the upthrust
to be human: a saint, a poet,
falls down;   chews the dustily
linoleum steps: to the slaughter pen

    goddam

black or green-pink or yellow skin
shatterburndeaths a Vietnam chitter
– at Gettysburg
they sawed bones without anesthetic
that's what they said

    son

wings at my heart
whose son dies?

    sonofabitch

the Powers waddling in fat
never missed a meal or a girl
bitchbitchbitch
coughing in a bare room
bandaging their rat-bites
in the fight for a lunch

    bitch

that's what they say

THE PENANCE

Inside the billboards
a barren steep follows
the line of a slum
apartment house.

I am thankful, at least,
for hill and height.
The chipping swallows flicking.

Shall I stop
running up the rotted stairs –
edging my shoes away from the vomit?
Join the fat whores
and the moonburned addicts
in the bleak elevator?

*

The things of the earth
are paired
with their opposites.
Seeds of the sunflower
get a start
in the shards
left by the wreckers.

Penciled by regret,
the outline of towns and faces –
peaches I bit into
and discarded.
The luck
I demolitioned!

In penance
I wrench from boulders,
cement-dust, and pebble
an uphill patch
and a water-dish for finches.

*

*Marigold, cornflower, lavender
and tansy.* Living past the blows
of empty bottles: a shower
from the dusty windows.
An occasional swallowtail
dries yellow wings, sips nectar.
Black stubby bees rumble,
stagger in the coreopsis powder.

*

Have I done wrong?
My fingers, in pulling up
hundreds of horsetails,
wire-feather, silicate-boned,
Coal-Age survivals,
are cut and corroded.
Their ghosts stalk my mind.
Their survivors will take over
the garden. Surviving my flesh
that nourishes flowers.

*

Tree-sparrow, street
sparrow, rosy housefinch
singing on any wire,

disregard
the stomp, the hack, the tarry fog
building a Freeway.
Walking their claws
among the fragrant stems;
are busy for crumbs.
Serene. The decorum
of the unthinking.
Teeter on the wet dish-rim.

They look up and fly.
I look up at the call
from an elderly drunk at a window.
"Lady! Pretty garden!"

TALKING OF YOU AND ME

You are happy nowhere (I'm talking to me).
Least heat and cold, and you hurl out your yell,
Continual summer your dreadful liberty
To cry for snow on a glittering hill;
And willful, will not look at people, a mob
In the thick streets, how grimy with life they are,
Equaling trees, a hinted moon, a silkworm web;
Their thoughts fine as air-color, if you would hear.
   And I shall never be filled and fortunate
   In the news my stumbling senses bring;
   Left to the chances of human wit
   I call the snake a rope and feel his sting,
   Till what I lost at birth I learn again:
   Anyone sings in the sparrow, things walk as men.

"M'INSEGNAVATE COME L'UOM S'ETERNA"

I

Waked, worked in the glassbanded buildings,
suffered the city.

As a wave and wetness
are one, and together –
you and I (transformed)
stroll – admire colonnade and belvedere –
along the lagoon.
               Grebe, geese, bathing.
               A gull's wingcrash into green water.
I don't forget.
Suburb from suburb
O you hurried me;
tugged, scolded.
Carried me the last miles of the mountain.

We endured. *We did not take one step.* We arrived.

II

Waylaid by morning   tiered and windowed.

A coot-flock   smooth   as smoke
flies squealing,
pecks grass.

YOU HAVE TAUGHT ME HOW MAN MAKES
       HIMSELF IMMORTAL:
he considers the shine

                    (pearls or apples)
of the world's plunder;
makes a choice.
                    (*Throw it!*)

He jumps into   the steaming chaos...

"I am, because I love."
                    (As raindrops and wetness
                    are one, and together.)

THE WINEGLASS

The mountainous housewall
porous unpainted brick
roughens the fist   pulls at clothing
Inside
on cheap tea   bread
and plummy jam
we keep growing

The stars
strike blue flecks
from a black cold –
I get tired
          of reading
and your arms
loop us tight

It is good here
a cedarwood palace
Starlight
          brims the wineglass
not sticky
leaving no stain

Well may we
look back to these nights
vanishing their silk
around a corner
              of the seasons
that fed us

ASTRONOMICAL NOTE

Venus, the Measurers said,
the octave of November 5
will be at the brightest.

Trailed by stars as their sparks burn out
she cuts a square from the night,
a house lit up for a revel;
she wakes me
and with her spoonful of honey
she feeds me;
smog, city lights, sink down
and thick clouds break into petals.

At the window
barely clothed   dawn-shivered
I sway in adoration.

It is written:
My sister is a jungle vine on Venus.

Lamenting the dark years
and nourished by them,
my tendrils cling to her radiant flesh.

LOVE IS A TRINITY

Nine candles, New Year's eve,
and so much light in us
we breathe and look with love.

Lost times, loveliness
and loneliness had called
our bodies to the kiss.

Now love's a trinity –
ourselves and That
which brings the worlds to be.

And we are the nine flames,
the roses and angels
adoring His names.

WAKE THE FLUTE

Green booth or golden, where we sing...
it is a silent snow-house now,
no longer home to the flute player
whose flute is charmed by icy sleep.

Let words for elms, their yellow and green
stripes of a kindergarten tiger,
be bonfires in the house of snow
to warm our blood and wake the flute.

And where we sing, the song-held leaves
dead underfoot and under snow
will shed their death to be the belled
green booth, or golden, the fluteplayer's home.

It is a silent snow-house...
bewitched by love to smell like spring.

THE LOSING

Bitter it was to me
That I could breathe sweet air,
That I could bear to breathe
The cold winds from the sea,

And you were lying – somewhere –
In the dull air of death.
No lily from the wood,
Nor pale-blue iris wreath,

Nor finch's running song,
To sweeten that dark drouth.
No laughter in the wheat
Nor its gold to curve your mouth.

Bitter and hard my bed. . . .
The clock gasped metal cries.
I watched the night grow old,
I saw the old moon rise

And thought of you as blown
Forever out to sea.
Innocent rose and bird
Were a bitterness to me.

AND JAYS FLY OVER

And from your distance   do you know
What wound I carry for the blow
Scattering you from room and door,
From days that sink, from nights that grow?

(Exquisite blue in lesser sky,
Overhead the young jays fly.)

Surely it is well with you there:
Endless dawn of flowering air,
More tender fingers offering new
And sweeter treasures for your stare?

(Blue jewels of a noonday river,
Two jays fly over.)

And you would rather be forsaken –
Unfastened from the noise of broken
Cries, the name that you surrendered
Plucks from a heart unhealed and shaken?

(Turquoise to cobalt, evening sky,
Overhead the young jays fly.)

Come in a dream – as I grieve sleeping.
Touch me and tell me I am keeping
Grief for your going from joy to glory;
Widen your wing. Then no more weeping.

(Dazzle and azure reweave the river,
Two jays fly over.)

NINE TIMES LONG AGO

The bush-primroses wake
Straw-crystalline, a square
Of petals, almost pure.
Lustrous, but a one-day sheaf
Like my day of love.

Tells my remembering wit,
"A long enchanted day
Though nine-times-long-ago
(Three times longer than that)
The seaweed scent of it."

By clock and calendar
I might tally a rhyme,
A seabird counting-time;
Year flying into year
Along the shelled shore.

Heart – clock – which tells true?
A long enchanted, one
Brighter than angels of sun,
(Nine-times-long-ago)
Was the love I knew.

NEW AS A WAVE

It is not as a stranger he will rise
Upon his bones to enter his new days.
(The features are a dialect I learned,
The voice, thought-colored, long years has laughed or moaned.)
A bird sheds feathers, a snake a used-up skin –
At last appears the man he was within.

I have made poems for his pleasure – was it his? –
His the deft fingers held me to the kiss?
Each self (and all) I loved, they bore his name
For me to hurt and heal in love's headlong game.
I never knew him though we loved in hell,
Made there our bed, dug there our living well.
I knew him and I knew him not – by faith
Defended each the other to the point of truth.

A beautiful power, a mercy of which I heard
Comes of him – *It is not my word but my Mother's word.*
I had no need of dying in order to be
A scholar of that white-fire theurgy.
Shells lie about to show that he has shed
Lifetimes in this life – was it with pain he played?
The youth astir in seeds, the childhood of rain,
Light's charming infancies – he had these for his own.

The changing river, in whose changes all are drowned,
Floats him, unwetted changeling, to high ground.
Sunwaxed, sunvarnished, the vines upon a wall
Announce a weepy world remains for all –
Not for him. New as a wave, newer than dew,
He brings a young landscape, a fifth season's snow:
His love unbewitching my mind and it knows
Him four-times-faithful by his feathered trees.

THE END OF AN EXILE

For a last look, you have climbed a hill – high
Among the hills along the river, like a carving
Of seated women drowsing over jars of oil.

The town-silhouette of ruined cupolas
Glows with the butter-yellow of bushes; comes out
Of the soot of a chimneyed noon to borrow
Crimson for alleys, the wine-splash of Virginia-vines.

From steeples like sticks, tones as tart as quince
Call back the heaped up, the forsaken days;
The millstacks are rose and red, like hollyhocks.

In the hill-ravines, the pepper-smell
Of fallen walnuts under falling leaves
Mingles with your thoughts ... you will leave your burdens
Here ... like broken shoes. ...

But remember a street, and the Lyre of Vega
You wandered for. ... The tufted titmouse calls,
You remember the known birds by their autumn song,

And how the birds flew, changing their colors
Like an emblem for the ways of water – and you cry
Farewell and the hills return the tolling cry.

VIGIL AFTER EQUINOX

The lake whispered to houses, sunk,
snatched from their rock. . . .
I looked with all my faces,
looked into wind-stir becoming any morning.

O it was cold . . . Good Friday wind
and caved two thousand years.
Through a lake-spray of blue wings
the feather-clarinets
cried the moments of sun's solo.

I lay with all my faces
pressed to the ice-burned rock.
Earth the Hunter said,
"Let rabbits dance in snow,
let the elk run till his hooves
strike grass from granite pebble –
I will catch you a golden fish
that has leaped the nine great heavens."

Sun said, "To dress the golden fish
I will churn a sweet butter of day."

From a midnight's ungold with-
holding, the ancestral wolf crept down,
(Weeping, little brother?)
and drank up all the lake;
in his ice-sharpened teeth
the lake-sunk stars were ringing:

"Nine times the nine white heavens
call the things that creep, run, fly.
Come to the fish-meal, eat from the tympani,
drink from the clashing cymbals."

I looked with all my faces.
The houses rose, shine-drenched,
the wolf ran at my side
through the Easter light of every morning.

A GARDEN'S SECRET

Tall from the split emerald of trees
The miles of fair atmosphere
Are brighter than smashed glass.

In a small garden I watch
Taking the sun a water
Beating an empty beach.

Garden. Neat as handkerchiefs
Monogrammed by a bird's
Curl of song under leaves.

Keeps a secret, won't talk
Of the God who is nested
Here, in the cool time to walk.

Nile-azure lily, marguerite
And roses, without my God
Of garden, border a blind street:

O Alph-Omega which lends
Me breath and power to feel
The Ghost-Who-Befriends,

Be nearer than the bee
Stumbling from petal to page
To finger, *O Reality!*

With all made things, all desire,
I am man, I must die.
Catch me to Thy mind of fire!

WINGSPREAD, WIDER THAN JOY

Green is a flame and chimes are a burning: Time burns
in a climate of treasons and we are betrayed
by a dog in our flesh. But what of that hollow
and the clear wings unfolded like a sky –
as if a slain jay had seen light, light,
beyond the bullet-blow and filled his feathers
and sunned himself forever in that light?

Always, all of us, we are in dusk:
deluded to name and fear a stumbling shadow –
yet see the bird! He has overflown
the cold delirium, around him flies
a dawn imagined in his lonely songs.

He fled into light, wingspread is wider than joy,
and tells how bluer than blue the true river flows,
dividing him from our mistaken night.

jay threw-out book

AM I AFRAID?

Miracle came to me over water.
By the luminous evening water
revelation came, a vesper sparrow
beautiful in the mirrored poplar.

Does it matter now whether I spread regal wings
or untie these tissues like a sack of chalk?

Kiss me in honor and fervor
and I clasp you, and loose you –
shower-scent, white peony;
good-by to velvet, and a closeheld love.

And this will be dying?
Whether by white fire or by white water
lost, cleansed, reassembled,
I am glad I shall be strange to myself,
a stranger to losing and having.

I shall carry no burden
over the midnight mountain.
Neither joy, nor stain, nor wildness
kept as scar of encounter.

Am I afraid?
      There was a miracle by evening water.

SO WIDE A WHITE ATMOSPHERE

When a truly northwind beats the spaces clear
Between twig and roof stark from a mountain wall,
Stripping a swaddled form to the admirable core –
Fire and water, at work in the lone cell –
It is a morning out of magic; no eyes
Ever took so purple a water, so wide
A white atmosphere; and yet the truth of my days
Marches confident into the daily cloud.

The arranged right words into my existence blow,
Break and uproot; busy to sweep and rinse,
A refreshing flood wherever it will go . . .
Charging the emptied self with excellence.
Words are. The right words act. They are declared
The Daughter of God. Our life walks in that word.

SONG BEFORE WINTER

Dry leaves are speaking
in the lessening light
as a longer night
to the earth is breaking.

Dear emerald of a planet –
mother and sister – receive
our praise and love
for each glowing minute.

Into sleep we go gaily
repeating the summerlong
bird and branching song,
tone by tone, slowly.

Ungrieved goodnight.   Remember
in the falling cold
our triumphant green and gold
and our sleep in amber.

THE LAZARUS CAROL
(to Carolyn Kizer)

And so we are awake.
Again the grave of sleep
Is robbed of Christ the sun.
We who hated our bodies,
Our habits,   our shabby names,
Now we must sin no more.

A river of winter sunrise
Like marred pearls or old paper,
Counting the Solstice hours
Flows from the side of a sun
Nailed to a hilltop pine.

We are redeemed for this:
To make choice shall we weep
Without reason, or wake
A dreadful reason for weeping.

Though the nations, ox and lamb
Garlanded with herbs,
Pretend that for a day
They are ruled from Bethlehem,
The nations pile new weapons
To build their hill of worship.
They set a threatening skull
In the straw of the Manger.

Not by nations but in single
Risings are the living dead

Baptized with the day-shine.
Each of us is chosen
For naming and praising the creatures
So lonely in their beauty,
Of the kingdom of creation –
Or for nothing Christ the sun
Had risen to the worlds.

NOTES

1. The translations in *Heliodora* originally appeared with added titles, as follows:

Author	First Line	Previous Title
Meleager	My flowerful Heliodora, wear	"The Last Garland"
Meleager	Tell fables, Lamp, O honey	"The Lamp, and Heliodora"
Agathias Scholasticus	My Heart, I am not fond of wine;	"I Am No Wine Bibber"
Agathias Scholasticus	(O city, where are thy temples packed	"Ilium"
Sappho	Show me in a dream, Queen Hera	"Queen of Heaven"
Leonidas or Meleager	*Death's freshest loot*	"Erinna"
Leonidas of Tarentum	*Before the dawn of your daybreak,* man,	"At Dawn of Every Daybreak"
Dioscorides	Sappho, all-ivied Helicon	"Immortal Sappho"
Nossis	O stranger if your stare	"Speaking of Myself"

With the exception of "The Lamp, and Heliodora," all are strict translations.

2. The Greek philosopher Plotinus strove to attain a state in which the self becomes united with the world-soul, the world-mind, and nature, succeeding three times during his life.

3. "Odyssey '69: A Book Review" was written after the poet received as a gift the book *Vacationing In Contemporary Greece* by D. V. Smith.

4. Philip McCracken (b. 1928) is a Pacific Northwest sculptor who works with cedar, juniper, stone, and steel to create images of birds, forest, and sea, depicting human states of mind. He is the poet's long-time friend.

5. Morris Graves (b. 1910), a Pacific Northwest artist, presently lives in Northern California. Drawing images from nature, his work is both personal and mystical.

ABOUT THE AUTHOR

Eve Triem was born in New York City on November 2, 1902. As an infant, she moved with her parents to California, where she grew up in San Francisco. While studying French at the University of California at Berkeley, she met writer Paul Ellsworth Triem, twenty years her senior, and after a four-week courtship they were married. During their fifty-two years together, they raised a son and daughter and made their home at various times in San Francisco, New York, and Dubuque, Iowa. Eve Triem was fifty years old when she embarked on the study of Greek at the University of Dubuque, a calling she continued to pursue in Seattle where she and her husband finally settled in the early sixties. Paul Triem died there in 1976 at the age of 94.

Eve Triem's poems have appeared in more than fifty magazines and ten anthologies, as well as in her previous six books. She has received the Taussig Award for French at U.C. Berkeley, 1924; the Charlotte Arthur Award, 1939; the League to Support Poetry Award, 1946; the Hart Crane and Alice Crane Memorial Award, 1965; a National Institute of Arts and Letters Award, 1966; and the Helen Bullis Award from *Poetry Northwest,* 1981. In 1968 she received a grant from the National Endowment for the Arts and in 1981 a Louisa Kern Publication Grant.

She has read her poems at universities and libraries across the country and conducted poetry workshops at the California Writers Conference, the University of Wisconsin, the University of Washington, the University of Washington Experimental College and the Seattle YWCA. In 1969-70 she lectured on e. e. cummings in western Washington public schools.

Design by Scott Walker
Type by Typeworks, Vancouver
Manufacturer: Thomson-Shore
Project editor for Dragon Gate was Joan Swift

Library of Congress Cataloging in Publication Data

Triem, Eve, 1902–
   New as a wave.

    I. Fortner, Ethel Nestelle. II. Title.
PS3539.R5A6 1984   811'.54   84-4171
ISBN 0-937872-24-5
ISBN 0-937872-25-3 (pbk.)